WELCOME TO
PASSPORT TO READING
A beginning reader's ticket to a brand-new world!

Every book in this program is designed to build read-along and read-alone skills, level by level, through engaging and enriching stories. As the reader turns each page, he or she will become more confident with new vocabulary, sight words, and comprehension.

These PASSPORT TO READING levels will help you choose the perfect book for every reader.

READING TOGETHER
Read short words in simple sentence structures together to begin a reader's journey.

READING OUT LOUD
Encourage developing readers to sound out words in more complex stories with simple vocabulary.

READING INDEPENDENTLY
Newly independent readers gain confidence reading more complex sentences with higher word counts.

READY TO READ MORE
Readers prepare for chapter books with fewer illustrations and longer paragraphs.

This book features sight words from the educator-supported Dolch Sight Words List. This encourages the reader to recognize commonly used vocabulary words, increasing reading speed and fluency.

Enjoy the journey!

ABDOBOOKS.COM

Reinforced library bound edition published in 2019 by Spotlight, a division of ABDO, PO Box 398166, Minneapolis, Minnesota 55439. Spotlight produces high-quality reinforced library bound editions for schools and libraries. Published by agreement with Little, Brown and Company.

Printed in the United States of America, North Mankato, Minnesota.
092018
012019

THIS BOOK CONTAINS
RECYCLED MATERIALS

LITTLE, BROWN

Hachette Book Group
237 Park Avenue, New York, NY 10017

Little, Brown and Company is a division of Hachette Book Group, Inc.
The Little, Brown name and logo are trademarks of Hachette Book Group, Inc.

Abridged Edition: September 2013
First published in hardcover in April 2004 as *The Extreme Team: One Smooth Move* by Little, Brown and Company

Library of Congress Control Number: 2018944560

Publisher's Cataloging-in-Publication Data

Names: Christopher, Matt, author. | Leonard, David, illustrator.
Title: The extreme team: skateboard moves / by Matt Christopher ; illustrated by David Leonard.
Description: Minneapolis, Minnesota : Spotlight, 2019. | Series: Matt Christopher sports readers
Summary: Charlie Abbott finally makes a friend after moving again, but when his skateboard disappears and his new friend is riding around on a board that looks similar to his, Charlie wonders if his life is about to become a disaster.
Identifiers: ISBN 9781532142574 (lib. bdg.)
Subjects: LCSH: Moving, household--Juvenile fiction. | Friendship in adolescence--Juvenile fiction. | Skateboarding--Juvenile fiction. | Theft--Juvenile fiction.
Classification: DDC [E]--dc23

Spotlight

A Division of ABDO
abdobooks.com

THE EXTREME TEAM
SKATEBOARD MOVES

by **MATT CHRISTOPHER**

illustrated by **David Leonard**

LITTLE, BROWN AND COMPANY
New York Boston

ABDO
Spotlight

Charlie skateboarded to a stop

on his new street.

He stomped his foot,

and the board popped up into his hand.

"Cool move," said a voice.

Charlie turned to see another boy

standing with one foot on his own skateboard.

"Your board is awesome!

Can I hold it?" asked the boy.

Charlie handed the boy his new

black-and-red board.

He had just moved to the neighborhood

and wanted to make friends.

The boy pointed to the "CA"

written on the skateboard.

"What does that stand for?" he asked.

"My name, Charlie Abbott."

"I am X," the boy said, handing back

Charlie's board.

"It is short for Xavier, Xavier McSweeney.

So, do you want to go to the skate park?"

"Sure!" said Charlie.

The two boys set off.

At the park, Charlie headed for the rails.

He popped an ollie

and jumped into the air with his board.

He held out his arms

and slid from one end of the rail to the other

before landing back on the ground safely.

"Nice!" X shouted.

Then, X jumped up,

sailed over the rail,

and landed with both feet on his board.

The boys took turns doing tricks.

Soon, it was time to go home.

"Your board is totally awesome!
I have to get mine in shape," X said,
looking at his old orange board.
"I think you were great with it," said Charlie.
"See you around!"

After dinner, Charlie helped his father

stack empty moving boxes in the garage.

They made the stack too tall, and it fell over.

Boxes landed everywhere!

Charlie's father took care of restacking them.

The next morning, Charlie did not see

his skateboard in the garage.

"Dad, did you move it when you were in there?"

Charlie asked.

"No, son, I did not see it," his dad answered.

That afternoon, Charlie went to the skate park.

There, he saw X doing a jump over a high rail.

As X popped an ollie,

Charlie saw a flash of black and red.

He could not believe it!

"X stole my skateboard!" he thought.

Charlie had an idea

to get X to confess to stealing his board.

He walked over to X.

"Do you want to meet tomorrow morning

to do some more boarding?"

"Sure, that would be cool!" X said.

"I will have to share your board with you,"

Charlie explained,

"because mine is missing."

He thought that would startle X.

"Okay, how about nine thirty?" X said.

X did not seem to be hiding anything.

"Maybe I am wrong," Charlie thought.

"Maybe he did not steal my skateboard!"

After breakfast the next day,

Charlie unpacked the box with his in-line skates.

He snapped them on and headed to the skate park.

He was the first one there when it opened,

but he was not alone for long.

A girl with dark hair skated up to him.

"Hi there!" she said.

"Did you just move here?"

"Yep," said Charlie.

"Cool, my name is Bizz.

That is short for Belicia."

Bizz headed to the half-pipe.

Charlie skated to the rails

to practice jumping over them.

An hour and a half later,

Charlie was still practicing.

Many more kids had come to the park,

but there was no sign of X.

Charlie was tired of jumping

and fed up with waiting.

He was sure now that X

had stolen his skateboard.

That must be why X had not come to the park.

"I am out of here," Charlie said to himself.

Charlie skated toward the exit gate.

He did not see X until he slammed right into him.

"You are still here!" X exclaimed.

"Surprised to see me?" Charlie sneered.

"Take a good look because the next thing

you will see is my back.

I know you stole my skateboard!"

He shoved X aside

and skated home as fast as he could.

By the time he got to his street,

Charlie was out of breath.

Without bothering to take off his skates,

he clumped across the lawn to a tree.

He sat down against the tree trunk

and drew up his knees.

Then he rested his head on his arms.

"There he is!

Under that tree!" he heard.

Charlie raised his head and looked around.

He saw Bizz with X and a few other kids

walking across the lawn.

Charlie wanted to run away,

but he had skates on.

He did not want to fall on his face

in front of the other kids.

"Charlie, I think there was a mix-up,"

said X.

He put his skateboard into Charlie's hands.

"Look," X said.

The board was black and red like Charlie's,

but the designs were different.

The board also had a nick in the nose.

It was not Charlie's board.

"Your board looked so cool," X said quietly,

"so I tried painting mine to look like it."

Charlie wanted to say he was sorry,

but all he could get out was, "Oh."

Then he asked,

"Why were you so late this morning?"

"I overslept.

I am sorry," said X.

"I am sorry I thought you stole my board.

Can we forget both things ever happened?"

asked Charlie.

X nodded.

Both boys smiled.

"There is still a mystery to solve," said Charlie.

"Where is my skateboard?"

"Where is the last place you saw it?" X asked.

"I put it in the garage," said Charlie.

The kids walked over to the garage.

Charlie flicked on the light.

No one saw a skateboard.

Charlie reached over to flick off the light,

but his hand hit the button for the garage door.

The sound startled Bizz.

She jumped and knocked into the stack of boxes.

"Look out!" Charlie shouted as cardboard fell.

"Wait a minute!" X said.

He went into the mess and felt around.

Suddenly, he broke into a huge smile.

He found Charlie's skateboard!

Charlie grabbed the board.

"How did it get stuck in there?" he asked.

"I think I can answer that question."

The children turned to see Charlie's father.

"I guess your skateboard got stuck under the

boxes when I was cleaning up the other day.

I am sorry!"

The kids looked at one another and laughed.

"No worries, Dad!" said Charlie.

Then he grabbed his board

and yelled to the other kids,

"Race you to the skate park!"